This book was drawn with pencils, sumi brushes, sumi ink,
and watercolors on watercolor paper.

Text, cover art, and interior illustrations copyright © 2022 by Mika Song

All rights reserved. Published in the United States by RH Graphic, an imprint of
Random House Children's Books, a division of Penguin Random House LLC, New York.

RH Graphic with the book design is a trademark of Penguin Random House LLC.

Visit us on the web and sign up for our newsletter! RHKidsGraphic.com • @RHKidsGraphic

Educators and librarians, for a variety of teaching tools, visit us at RHTeachersLibrarians.com

Library of Congress Cataloging-in-Publication Data is available upon request.
ISBN 978-0-593-47972-8 (hardcover) — ISBN 978-0-593-47973-5 (lib. bdg.)
ISBN 978-0-593-47974-2 (ebook)

Designed by Patrick Crotty

MANUFACTURED IN CHINA
10 9 8 7 6 5 4 3 2 1
First Edition

A comic on every bookshelf.

A **NORMA** AND **BELLY** BOOK

PIZZA
MY HEART

mika Song

Also by Mika Song

———

Tea with Oliver
Picnic with Oliver

Norma and Belly Books

———

Donut Feed the Squirrels
Apple of My Pie

chapter 1

4

7

chapter 2

chapter 3

29

Chapter 4

This is the home of Tomato, the meanest cat in town.

Chapter 5

chapter 6

69

chapter 7

Chapter 8

Mika Song is a children's author who makes stories about
sweetly funny outsiders. She has illustrated several books
including A Friend for Henry by Jenn Bailey, which received
a Schneider Family Honor from the American Library
Association. She is the creator of the Norma and Belly series,
which includes Donut Feed the Squirrels, an Eisner Award
nominee, and Apple of My Pie.

She loves drawing on paper and meeting young readers. Her
favorite pizza is the one she is about to put in her mouth.

🐦 📷 @mikasongdraws
mikasongdraws.com